ANCI
BOO

The Final Frontier

Edited by Neil Day

First published in Great Britain in 2001 by
ANCHOR BOOKS
Remus House,
Coltsfoot Drive,
Peterborough, PE2 9JX
Telephone (01733) 898102

HB ISBN 1 85930 814 7
SB ISBN 1 85930 819 8

FOREWORD

The challenge was set within these pages - to write a story with a beginning, a middle and an end in only 50 words; and so the mini-saga was born. Lots can be said in a few words - enabling a brief exchange between reader and writer, creating a bond as characters and stories unfold between the lines.

Read on to enjoy the very best in a huge variety of stories, tales, sagas and fables, sure to demand and delight all who read *The Final Frontier.*

Neil Day
Editor

Contents

The Poems

It's A Slug's Life

'I'll get there if it kills me,' were the last words of the slimy slug as he sniffed the irresistible smell of beer, put in the jar for that very purpose. He slid as fast as his slime could be produced, to plop into the beer and drown. Ah bliss!

Brian Kelly

Eagle Of Gold

Beckoning, shining golden against the blue of sky,
they honoured it with soul and life.
To lose it was worse than death.
Disdaining pain, gore and barbarian ferocity,
they stabbed with sword and bludgeoned with shield
until they sheltered under its wings. They held it secure;
Rome's Eagle of Gold.

Ron Greer

Until

'He'll be here soon.'
The crowd gasp in anticipation.
Push turns to shove.
I feel my throat dry up, I'm sweating,
and now claustrophobia is setting in.
'He's here.'
He opens the door and suddenly
Stampede
The January sale begins.

Julie Murphy

A Day To Live Or A Day To Die

The gladiator stood over his quarry with his sword at his throat.
Both were breathing heavily, their hearts thumping in their breasts.
Sweat stung the victor's eyes, as he looked at the Roman Emperor.
Would his thumb turn up or down?
He prayed not to take another life . . . his prayers were answered.

Gillian Mullett

Goodnight

When it's time for beddy-byes
And teddy's cuddled right
Fairy tales and lullabies

It's time to say: goodnight
I'll stroke her little, angel face
Clasp my hands and pray
That God will grant me all the strength
To face another day.

Roger Brooks

Phipps

Phipps the publican's wife nagged him about
Lucille's behaviour; he was past caring.
A stray customer started the pianola.
It stopped. Lucille kicked it and it started again.
Her boyfriend with his sneering profile
came into the cellar. Phipps pushed his face in
a barrel and he drowned.

A J Vogel

Evanescence

Welling hysteria rising in inverse proportion to depression, he turned in
trepidation to the mirror, seeing even less than before. Was this a trick mirror?
Was he losing his peripheral vision? Was he somehow one of the Undead from
Dracula stories? An abysmal dread obsessed the soul of Dorian Gray.

Patrick Brady

Saga C21

I was on planet Mars
In the year of 2832
I caught an express train
Across Mars City Twenty two
Skyscrapers tall as can be
Everywhere my eye could see
Passing through a small station
Then through a giant skyscraper
The train 'took' to the skies
And landed on moon Phobos.

H G Griffiths

A Child's Nightmare

It tormented her nightly and once again
she found herself trapped, all avenues
of escape cut off. Fear tied her stomach
in knots and rivulets of sweat slid down
her silken cheek. The implements of her
torture were laid in a neat row. There
was no escaping . . . bath time.

Angela Barrett

The Long Way Forward

It seemed miles, there was nothing in front of me, nothing behind me,
to the right there were roses, to the left there were trees,
a fountain ran with water.

The birds were singing, the sky was blue, the sun was setting,
then suddenly I saw it my front door!

Elizabeth Hart

What Bill And Jan Saw That Day

Bill and Jan went mountain climbing Mount Snowdon,
cloudy day they climbed so far, Jan slipped she
screamed, Bill shouted 'Hold on tight, try and lift
yourself up.' At last she gasped. Bill and Jan
climbed the top of the high mountain. Both looked
up, heaven opened, a bright rainbow they saw.

Christine Shurey

Desperate

Panic, sweating on upper lip, grasping the steel rails, she hauled herself up the
steps, pounding the tarmac enveloped by the noisy, smelly, roaring train in the
cold morning air.
Clattering down to the platform, faint but pushing doors, right, sharp left and
panting, finally locking the loo door!

Jean Horsham

A Living Hell

(Respectfully dedicated to both sides of the family)

From choice they all wanted a quick exit.
Some looked left, others right.
Still more backwards and forwards,
Up and down -
Side to side -
Some time later the rescue party arrived with boundless patience.
For even they, themselves, could be wrong!
Is there no end to this maze?

M D H Stalker

An Anchor Books Anthology

Rising Agent

It was Liberation Day celebrated after five years of enemy occupation.
The lucky ones swooped upon chocolate bars, chewing gum and other long
forgotten luxuries, thrown into the joyous crowds by our liberation forces.
In triumph, I carried home a humble packet of baking powder disregarded by
the bounty hunters.

Daphne Kirkpatrick

The Final Frontier

One Dark And Stormy Night

The wind howled through the trees
snapping branches, each gust bringing
lashing rain down on his back.

He stumbled forward, wet and weary
when distantly, home appeared, the welcome
sight spurring him onwards.
He pushed open the door, black nose and
whiskers twitching hungrily calling
'Is tea ready, Mrs Badger?'

Jill Barker

The Prisoner

'Pig-swill,' Peterson screamed, hurling the bowl at the Warden,
its sodden contents splattering her uniform.
Her last day on Death Row for Murder 1.
Suddenly the Warden's phone rang.
'Brace yourself Peterson, you've got a reprieve from the Governor.'
In tears on her knees, Peterson shouted
'Thank you God.'

Carole Hanson

Smuggler's Cave

The waves lapped against the shore and above this
I could hear voices coming from within the caves.
Curiosity won and I peeped quietly in. To my
surprise, smugglers were unloading gold, silver and
jewels, while drinking heartily from the many casks
of wine. I ran and ran, then awoke.

Peggy Howe

The Adoption

The postman fumbled, pulled out an envelope
and popped it through our letterbox.
'It's from the Adoption Society darling, it says
Your application for adoption has been accepted.'
The wife looked shocked.
At the Adoption Society our little fellow stood waiting,
nose pressed against the window.
His tail wagging furiously.

Merv Pack

The Final Frontier

A Child's Awe Of The Thames, At Henley

A summer's day.
Our annual visit to my Henley aunt, almost
ended in my demise!
The wide challenge of the river; a
swimmer, aged nine, clung tenaciously to
sweeping, far-bank willows, regaining her breath!
Worried mother and aunt, paced the bank;
witnessed small child's safe return, unharmed,
breathlessly, prayerfully . . .

Julia Yeardye

A Picture Of Painted Folk Stood Under A Tall, Dark Tree

They were visiting the witch doctor, who was about to tell them their future. Amongst them stood a tall girl, she was due to have her baby. Bang, then thud, then ouch the girl had gone into labour. The wizard chanted his song to drown out her shouts of pain and anguish.

Safely delivered.

Jennifer Dunkley

Psychic

I did not have a crystal ball so I could hopefully see my future.
So I filled a glass bowl with water (as a substitute)
Then darkened the room.
I concentrated hard for some time;
At last, there it was, magical, mystical writing,
What was the message? *Pyrex.*

Yvonne Magill

An Anchor Books Anthology

A Day At Ambleside, Lead To Excitement Of A Hound Trail

We joined a group of people, intently watching a
lone figure weaving his way up the fell, leaving a
trail of aniseed.
With excited yelps the dogs got the scent, then
whoosh, up and down and round they sped.
When eventually the winner came into view, the
proud owners were ecstatic.

Elizabeth Myra Crellin

The Final Frontier

The Ordeal

I'll show you, he thought, as full of apprehension and heart pounding, he
waited for the signal.
When it finally came, his reaction was automatic. Both feet slammed down on
the controls. His passenger hurtled forward against his restraints.
'Excellent' said the shaken driving examiner handing him his pass slip.

Don Woods

Dreaming Silently

She was hurting inside, but scared to show it,
she didn't want feelings turning into an
argument like they normally did, all she
wanted was a chance to do the things
she wanted together. Surely he would
understand, but who knows, she'd rather
carry on and live in his world. Dreaming.

Michelle Barnes

Ignorance Can Provide Security As Well As Bliss

The North Wind blew with triumphant vigour. Two bleating sheep ran to the
Oak for shelter. With howls of fury the gale tore at the tangled branches. The
tree shuddered then crumpled southwards across the boundary lane. Two
bewildered sheep slithered from severed roots to the safety of familiar green
field.

Margaret Connolly

Wicked William

William wandered into the whispering wood at dawn, where Walter the wizened dwarf was whistling while he worked. William waited a while and watched the dwarf weaving a wonderful web.
'Welcome to my whitewashed dwelling,' whispered the dwarf.
Walter waved a wand, whirling the web towards William who was whisked away.

Catherine Craft

The Private Eye

A call from a woman questioning her husband's fidelity took me to a Long Island pizzeria, where he met a couple of dark-suited guys to whom he spoke in hushed tones. His wife's phone call led to me getting a promotion and him in the witness security protection programme.

Simon Kirkpatrick (14)

The Conqueror

He paused in his pursuit as his target was now in sight. Weapons at the ready, one final effort and the prize would be his. He made his move and dealt the final blow. His victim was despatched. As was his custom, he carried the body home - cat and mouse.

Jennifer Houghton

The Final Frontier

The Lake Of Dreams

'Where a wizard of dreams
in a world of frozen liquid glass
with razor shadows, wind and spark
floats sleepers, taken, by midnight's deep and magic's dark;
A supernatural enchanted chased sleep.
Magic, little and big, Moorland legend speaks
and of realms beyond
where rises phantom stranger,
the amber peaks . . .'

Paul Holland

An Anchor Books Anthology

The Calming Of The Bear

The large bear lurched forward, eyes flashing,
its temper aroused. A fierce growl started to
form in its throat. One man raised his fist,
another kicked out at it. A third man picked
up a stone. The girl spoke to it, soothingly,
calmly. The huge animal retreated, its anger
subsiding.

Sheila Tatem

Too Late

'What's he doing?'
'He's planting something.'
'Let's go and look.'
'It's a silver birch.'
'Why are you planting it?'
'My wife had cancer.'
'Sorry.'
'It was her time to go.'
'Dogs will widdle on it.'
'She'd laugh at that.' (Tears)
'Did you love her?'
'Not enough. Sadly it's too late.'

Peter Murphy

Room 102

A voice cracked, indistinguishable words became audible. 'He's in intensive care.' She sounded fragile. I let the answerphone take the call. I should see him, though there'd be no recognition, no response; he's beyond that now. Unable to survive without artificial life; on release he relapses, as his heart collapses.

Amy Phillips

Anticipation

Hush, listen, the sound of silence was amazing. Clouds scurried silently across the sky. The air electric with anticipation, the children waited. Straining to hear the slightest sound. Excitement almost visible to touch. Then, the very faintest sound of tinkling bells. The room erupted. Silence no more . . . Santa is on his way.

Sheila A Waterhouse

Buttonmoon Balderdash

When I walk alone at night, a biconcaved moon lights my way,
my imagination runs wild, with the thought of alien life forms from far away.
I would often truly love to be indoors, instead of having thoughts of other life
forms upon which I thought I had hit. Today I dismiss these thoughts as
fallacious, human twaddle (but then again was it?).

John P Evans

Eric The Judge

Look who has been caught taking something that is not his, Eric laughed, a sword and axe but gets caught once he has got them. The slave did not look very happy as he stood before Eric. 'Into the snake pit,' said Eric. Let's see what happens.

Keith L Powell

Wisdom Is Better Than Strength
(Ecclesiastes In The Old Testament)

A wise man lived in a small city,
with few inhabitants.

A powerful King came against that city;
surrounded it and built fortifications
round it, so that there seemed no
hope for the terrified inhabitants.
Then the poor man used his wisdom
and by his wise planning, saved that city.

Frida Harris

The Final Frontier

Life

Through the town, working the traffic, I went like the wind, left at the lights, I looked behind, I was being followed. I could go no faster, then I saw it, the fire, we stopped and went to work. One more life saved, it's worth driving a fire engine.

Peter Allen

Halfway House

It was a very sinister house,
when they entered the front door it
seemed as if someone flicked their hair.
Inside was a long hall, they went along
that's when they heard this little boy
and girl laughing.
It was haunted, it had been for years,
but it's to be sold.

Elizabeth Barrs

Conductor

He wields his keys like a jailer and highlights striking castles in the atmosphere. The strings plant the major scaffolding.

He pulls the audience in hiding with nerves distant from his pleasure, vibrant colours follow the flames in composed frames.
Fashions never intrude from their dungeons.

Marylène Walker

Opening Night

'Overture and beginners' announced the voice over the intercom.
Voices subsided as people headed towards the stage. As the
overture began minds whirled over lines, hearts pounded and
mouths dried - just first night nerves. The curtain rose as the
overture reached its climax. Now, it was on with the show.

Katherine Parker

The Final Frontier

A Diary Of Anguish

Captured, dirty and lonely, I lie in the darkness, dying of hunger.
My skin is lank and creased out with wrinkles and my throat is sore and dry,
not uttering a word. My clothes lie on my body as comfort of which they
aren't.

Shelina Alagh

Two Strange Coincidences

I dangled my first fishing line over Cromer pier on holiday
200 miles from home. I made a catch and tugged, but *snap* it went and my 10
year-old heart broke too. Next day we bumped into neighbours from home who
had been fishing - and caught my line.

David Varley

The Final Frontier

Victim

Scurrying through the shadows, hopelessly aware that something is following.
Jumping and weaving around objects that appear in his path. Realising that
every step taken, the distance between him and the stranger reduces. Lacking
energy, slowly he stops. Heart beating, faster, facing, thumping. Darkness.
Mouse nil, bird of prey one.

Jacqueline Emma Aldridge

The Romans

They had walked foot across land and really for their armour, they were rather grand. They sailed in ships and fought. Treasures and jewels is what they brought, they were obviously not poor. The Romans had not really thought of the bad things they had taught.
They made war worldwide.

Archana

The Dawn Avenger

First the menacing creak of the stairs then the bedroom door opened.
Shivering, he pulled the pitiful protection of bedclothes around him knowing
there was no escape. The agitated breathing drew nearer and then the dreaded
words 'Get up, I won't tell you again, you'll be late for work.'

Joyce Atkinson

A Ball Of Fire

As we ran across the Tyne Bridge, the squealing sound was getting louder,
police cars to the rescue of a burning tanker which blocked the road. We
helped by holding the children who were shaking with shock. Firemen and
Ambulance men struggled to control the situation.

Kenneth Mood

The Final Frontier

Presenting Santa

Slowly Santa slipped down the smokestack. The suspended stockings shuddered as Santa suddenly stopped. He shook the soot off his scarlet suit and stealthily slipped his fist into the sack of festive surprises. Santa selected a spherical present for Saskia, a soft, squishy surprise for Sam and a small, shiny 'something' for Sarah. He smiled to himself, visualising the spectacular scene of ecstatic faces. Sarah was sleeping soundly, snug in her sleeping bag on the sofa. She sat up suddenly in a state of semi-sleep, shocked to see Santa placing the stuffed stockings on the mantelpiece.
'S-S-Santa?' she stuttered, 'Is it Christmas so soon?' Hesitating at first, Santa whispered softly, 'Yes, it is.'

Dawn Abrahams (11)

The Dead Of Night

Trouble sleeping, hearing noises. Firstly a creaking on the stairs, then movement in the attic, sounds like objects being moved about. Petrified still listen-
ing, the curtains swish and now there's a tapping on the back door. After
investigating, feeling stupid, really - it's only the house settling down for the
night.

Bernice Sharpe

Imagine

Not caring how could he. Carefully the lilies placed, alone, uncaring,
devoid of pot or moisture.
To deprive her of the honour of the fresh bloom of youth.
Not unfeeling, not uncaring, the opposite feelings they had engendered.
'Plastic' he said aloud.
'Plastic lasts forever.'

Jean Daisy Bradley

The Prowler

It was a very cold night and the moon was shining high in the sky. Casting an eerie glow over the frost-covered ground which was sparkling like little diamonds as I stood there wondering how the moon which was right above my head could be shining over other countries as well. It was very quiet, in the stillness, I could hear the twoo-twit-twooing of an owl. Then I heard something closer, a rustling from under the neighbour's hedge, I think it was a hedgehog. I ignored it and went back to my sky gazing then there it was again the rustling. I could feel my heart pounding then suddenly, whoosh. A black and white shape flashed past my feet, I was relieved to discover it was only a cat out on its nightly prowl after a little mouse.

Jean Logan

The Final Frontier

Unfamiliar Territory

The beast stared at him, seemingly content to wait him out on this plateau of
silence. Scared and angry all at once, he knew any movement could invite
catastrophe.
A veteran member of the team appeared at his side. She whispered in his ear
'Just hit the *Clear* button, love!'

Perry McDaid

Bee-Trayed

The bee had been after the honeysuckle, but the wisp of wild cotton reached its target first. Unknowingly it flew across the bee's path. Now fluffy, white fibres totally engulfed the bee. The fate of this buzzing, swirling marshmallow was sealed.

Paul Harvey Jackson

Stormy Weather

It was raining heavily as I drove carefully, avoiding the puddles
Towards the harbour. Gradually it stopped, the sun came out
And a lovely rainbow appeared. I reached the harbour in time
To greet my family aboard their yacht 'Stormy Weather'
As it entered calmer waters before raining again.

Elisabeth Morley

Little Creature Of Habit

Each morning he greets me with his chirpy song
Pecking up his breakfast from the window ledge.
Then off he goes to his birdy business whatever that may be.
I'm aware of his presence as evening approaches
He chirping away in my old fir tree,
Goodnight my friend, Robin Redbreast.

Gladys C'Ailceta

The Battle

The air was thick with clashing armoury
and blood ran too fast. Sir Oswald said
his fine force could end all wars, Sir
Henry wiped a tear away for he foresaw more
great charges still and lands forsaken and
and bereft of valour in strange future schisms
he could not describe.

John Amsden

An Anchor Books Anthology

Close Encounters

He leant over her,
So close she could hear him breathing,
She could smell peppermint on his breath.
The light shone brightly,
Forming a halo around him
She lay there nervously.
He tried to relax her, smiling sweetly.
'Okay Judie, see you in six months.'
Judie left the dentist's relieved.

Kathryn Rees

Hope

They thought it would never happen, as they had tried
everything they knew, but they waited patiently until
at last they saw the sign.
So they nurtured it, they tended it lovingly, they slowly
watched it grow.
Until the day it finally came.
A beautiful baby boy.

Kathleen Morris

A Weekend Break

Weekend break essential we depart for the ferry to Amsterdam.
Arrive at the hotel ready for a 'Grand Slam'
friend descending gracefully down the coach steps
misses her footing, falls over onto the garden.
Screams in agony, off we travel to casualty department
X-rays confirm a broken ankle joint.
What a jinx!

Mary Wood

The Final Frontier

Rough-Paved, The Way To Paradise

After months of training for the Olympic Games, his national anthem being
played, he stands on the centre rostrum with a gold medal, Paradise gained.
Later having refreshing shower, alarming lump discovered!
Paradise lost.
Anxious day, the sleepless night, hospital visit arranged.
With the consultant's 'Not malignant,' behold!
Paradise regained.

George Nicklin

My Joy

The pain was very slight,
I didn't know what to expect,
Time was pushing on
The pain was getting worse
My husband ran around in a panic
Traffic was bad
My baby is perfect!

Sharon Hughes

Deathwatch

She sat nervously waiting for her husband, he had never been gone so long in the forest before. She began to worry, she had seen it on the news, husbands and wives going missing and then being found dead in the forest. Then she remembered the missing persons' loved ones deranged reports of hearing a gentle buzz until they found out the loved one was dead. Suddenly she heard a soft buzz, her mind clicked - she dashed to the forest, afraid of what was coming but anxious to get there in time before it happened. She saw the body - a knife through her husband. Then she felt a cold, piercing pain in her back. The Deathwatch Beetle had struck again!

Frederick Burdon

The Dressing Gown

Its body swayed, its arms clenching at me, I hide beneath my bed then I look out in fear. The cloaked body started towards me. I threw a cushion at it, it made no difference. The door opened, the light turned on! I find the cloaked figure was my dressing gown.

Christopher Marshall (11)

Fast

Whirling, twirling, speeding along - white
blue racing by dodging, weaving from the
terrifying bangs of the guns.

Chasing us as we sped along losing the
bandits far behind.

Stopping slowly on a ship - the quick air
war was now over and my jet was in a
hanger.

Ben Glaister (11)

Melting

We were playing outside. It was freezing.
We were making a big ball, then a medium ball,
Then a small ball. We put rocks in the small ball,
Sticks in the middle ball, a carrot in the small ball.
Out came the sun - it went. The snowman was gone.

Callum Kerry (10)

The Walk

There I walked nearer and near.

Someone went in. I felt very scared
in case we had to do something hard.

Then someone shouted and I hurried
into the classroom and I was told to
write a mini saga.

Stuart Keegan (10)

School

We were in the playground, I heard the bell go, we all ran as fast as we could. I
could smell it. Suddenly I tripped, other people ran past.
I could still smell it. It was like I was at home.
Finally I got there. It was lunchtime.

Edward Keyes (11)

The Final Frontier

Top Speed

As we raced down the highway he was taking me somewhere. Eventually we reached an abandoned warehouse. Suddenly he heard a noise. The noise sounded like a screech and in the background you could hear it was getting closer. Frightened, his face went pale. He ran out of the building at the speed of light. There were police everywhere.

James Craven (10)

The Light

I lay down and then I saw it. It was round, long and it was light.
It was coming closer and closer. I thought it looked like a flying saucer.
I was scared, frightened, alone but then I opened my eyes and it was
my light bulb moving.

Callum Ruffman (10)

The Game

Everyone was nervous. It was the first for all of us.
The others were waiting. It started, it flew up and then fell.
We grabbed it and then they came. They missed it.
Another person caught it. He saw them coming.
He fled. He touched down the rugby ball.

Nicholas Dowie (10)

The Sleeping Policeman

We were watching the policeman as we walked along the street.
He was inches away from being run over by a car for he was in the road.
Then a man said 'Why are you staring at a little speed bump?'
It was a sleeping policeman.

Alan Watkinson (11)

The Living Dead

He'd been away for five years! He went home. It was very cold.
His mum was sitting there. 'Hi' she said. 'Hi, Mum, you look rough!'
'Go and ring Michelle.'
He rang. 'Hello, hi, it's Bill, I'm at Mum's. She looks rough doesn't she!' 'Are
you mad! She's been dead for two years.'

Andrew Hall (11)

Tig!

The enemy was charging after me. I was running,
I was very tired in this chase,
I could barely lift my legs.
I started seeing stars with faces.
My friends froze quite still.
The monster was charging at me,
I was helpless then 'Tig!'
I was stuck in the mud.

Robert Harris (10)

The Big Mistake

She moved closer inch by inch closing the gap.
Closer, closer, keeping still when it moved.
It ran away, she bridged the gap as silently as possible,
Metres away getting closer.
She snapped a stick, it ran away!
She pounced, but missed it.
The lioness had missed her kill.

Cornel Dixon (11)

The Rock 'N' Roll Singer's Walk In A Pub

After the rock 'n' roll singer didn't drink as he described his space station project because he drives. He walked down an art exhibition corridor containing drawings, disasters, war, comedy, space, notices, transport and Mars; to be a comedian on stage, socialise and market children's picture story books in a pub.

Darth Rambo (B A Hons)

Fotheringay

The executioner stooped over the kneeling body.
It had taken two clean swipes of the axe.
The ladies in waiting wept silently.
Her little cairn terrier whimpered.
The axeman congratulated himself on his task.
A herald declared 'So perish the foes of Lady Elizabeth.'
The Queen of Scots was dead.

Alan Pow

But Tonight Was Different

She turned around, to be caught in aspiration,
who was it staring in her mirror, which stood opposite the window?
It was pitch-black outside, Ann never closes her curtains whilst she writes
poems but tonight was different . . .
yet there was another person's reflection staring back.
- Surely that isn't me?

Ann Worrell

The Final Frontier

Bitter-Sweet Victory As The World

Watched And Waited

Victory was seized, by human error blow in the twelfth hour.
Significant calculations made hands busy,
as the opposition viewed one another.
The loser would not yield,
Rules were cast aside, days stretched into weeks.
The judge's decision was final.
America's election fiasco,
year 2000 finally came to an end.

Ann G Wallace

New And Olde

Times changed, no music, birds, trees
Land just a barren desert with a spaceship for a house,
I hate it, tell me I'm dreaming, let me wake up in the past, in your arms,
I want family round me and 'Old' Christmas's,
The way life was, I can always dream.

Lucy Lee

The Final Frontier

Ghosts

My fellow traveller sat opposite me in the train, stood up and said,
'Here mate, do you believe in ghosts?'
'No, mate!' I replied. 'No,' he said, 'Neither do I.'
He then stood up and disappeared, leaving no sign that
he'd ever been there at all.

Mick Nash

Peace At The Bottom

She stopped her car at the edge of the cliff, finished off the whisky bottle and
accelerated hard. Her car flew off the edge towards the sea as her life - her
memories - flashed before her. She greeted death and by the time she hit the
bottom, had found her peace.

Sarah Patterson

Fateful Date

Waiting under the tower for his date to arrive
the young man felt good to be alive.
Noticed his date, looking good enough to eat,
then the blood, underneath his feet.
Through his body was the clock tower hand,
struck down by the grim reaper's speciality,
the one o'clock scythe.

Andy Monnacle

The Homecoming

Two minuses make plus. Why remember a childhood teaching at a time like this? Returning late from a clandestine meeting with his latest ladylove, he had discovered his wife in the arms of his best friend. Two minuses . . . he had never really understood why. What's more, it no longer mattered!

Mary Ryan

Dreams Come True

She worked very hard with her husband to bring up their family.
But always longed to have her very own car.
Then it happened on her birthday,
there stood a red, shiny car in the driveway.
A present from the family and her dream had come true at long last.

Hazell Dennison

The Creature

I was trembling as I opened the door.
It scratched at me as I forced him out of the cage.
Its fur all scruffy, its claws deadly.
It was angry, I woke it up and sought revenge,
It sunk its teeth into me.
'You bad hamster,' I yelled in pain.

Kathleen Ingleby (13)

The Fortress

The harvest was safely stored in the fortress - time to relax.
Then suddenly the message came - Invasion!
The queen sent out the army to repel and defend.
Too late.
Smoke filled the air as the roof disappeared.
A figure loomed overhead and said
'Blimey - plenty of honey this time!'

Vivian Finlay

Prompt Thinking

Returning from shopping, people were running towards me shouting
'Stop that thief,' obviously he was making for a parked car
alongside of me.
As he neared, I threw my laden shopping trolley
at him causing his downfall.
He was caught, charged, found guilty, police commending me
on my brave, prompt action.

Kathleen Jones

It Would Appear To Have Been My Lucky, Lucky Day

I went to hang-glide like many times before but this time I ended on the floor
with my safety strap broken.
I watched it hurl its life away without me into the affray and not once did it
consider me.
It splashed head on into the docks of the bay!

Brad Boyd

Christmas Day

All the children were asleep,
The snow lay crisp and deep,
Mince pies for Santa, sat under the tree,
Where presents and parcels are soon to be,
Morning breaks, children excitedly rush,
Busy chatter steals the morning hush,
Smiles fill this land on this special day.

Peter Littlefield

The Cross

David was a young soldier captured by the Japanese
forcibly laboured on The Burma Railway.
Every mile of track was marked by graves of soldiers
Human remains laying the foundation,
Outbreak of cholera, death took its toll.
Bedraggled soldiers moved further along the track
carrying dead comrades.
Suddenly David saw a cross symbolising triumph amidst tragedy.
With determination David survived, became a great preacher.

Frances Gibson

Chain Reaction

Junk mail - who needs it?
The final straw was 'Smutty Faxes Ltd'. It took a while to devise my revenge
but tonight I hit the headlines: 'Chain letter threatens world advertising
industry'. People power - deadly effective.
It's been so successful, I'm looking for marketing staff now to
keep it running!

David Gasking

The Final Frontier

Rescue

The golden blonde slid from the rock, disappearing beneath the waves. An arm entangled in seaweed rose above the surface of the sea, only to disappear again. He swam to her rescue, fighting the strong current and as he pulled her free from the water he noticed the fishes tail.

M Riches

The Reader

He sat - relaxed in his chair, his mind
filled with the images formed by the
pages that lay before him, his mouth
forming every syllable that his eyes had
followed from the very first paragraph,
his imagination building the framework
line by line - his attention gripped to the
very end.

Marc Tyler

The Final Frontier

Casabianca's Curse

While playing cricket next door, a boy
feels thirsty, runs home, gulps glassfuls
and rushes out. His bed-ridden father,
late with his medication, summons him
back. His ears get tugged. He turns cold
and curses Dad. The man dies shortly.
A bed-ridden old widower now hourly
weeps his decades-old misdeed.

Kopan Mahadeva

Sightseer

Seeing a canopy of tents was fantastic, the sight he had been hoping
to see for so long was now there in front of him. Food and water would, no
doubt, be available and plentiful. Then the mirage faded and he realised he was
going to die in the desert.

Andy Monnacle

Foolish Decision

The new mother sighed, baby screamed, the nurse was happy to
have a job she loved. The father was absent, having showed
no interest from the moment he heard the news. Later in life he
would bitterly regret his foolish decision, his longing to see his
child was torturous.

Danny Coleman

Discovery

What is this? The hand pulled my ear until I gave up the note, I had waited months for a reply . . . He read it aloud *I love you!* My face turning scarlet. My grandchildren love to hear about my embarrassment - we eventually got married - Sir was our guest.

John of Croxley

Vote Of Confidence

The bridegroom stood shivering at the altar.
He wondered even now if he was doing the right thing.
Where was Yvonne? Her lateness bothered him, acutely.
Did she also have qualms? Mostly about Kevin Noakes.
But no. Yvonne, his mother's pleasure illuminated the
church as she entered and he was reconciled.

Ruth Daviat

The Dream

He struggled desperately to waken from the dream
His lungs demanding air.
He realised in shock this really was happening.
He felt lips on his and air entering his mouth.
His eyes opened slowly, incredulous at the blurred scene,
The girl in white asked his name,
shocked he realised he could remember nothing.

Terry Daley

Will It Be On The News?

The boat tossed. The helicopter hovered as the winchman
descended in spray from the rotors.
On the beach speculation raced through the crowd.
'Was it a drugs' raid?'
'Perhaps a casualty on board.'

The Coastguard vehicle sped along the beach,
Eagerly questioned the driver ended rumours,
'Sorry, just an exercise . . .'

Di Bagshawe

The End Of Paradise

Volcanic eruptions ripped apart this
ancient continent, sending it into the
crashing waves of the Atlantic Ocean.
A wondrous civilisation 12 miles wide,
exploding in its death throes, loudly
shattering into millions of pieces, as
this once mighty kingdom, finally blew
itself out of existence. Now Atlantis
was gone forever.

Christopher Higgins

A'Hunting We Will Go

Walking dog in parkland, elegant lady passed by.
Silver fox fur, adorning neck, tail dangling behind.
Suddenly, lead wrenched away
Terrier leapt, bushy tail in mouth, shaking till it fell
Lady frightened, I took home.
I'm lonely no more. Dog forgot
Married bliss now my lot.

Ivy Lott

On The Lake

As we sailed, we fell asleep and there came down a storm of wind on the lake.
We shouted, 'Master, we perish!' Then he arose and rebuked the wind, there
was a calm. I wondered and said 'Even the winds and water obey Him. What
manner of man is this?'

Ebenezer Essuman

The Final Frontier

The Late Arrival

The night seemed long, never ending.
In the corner the woman groaned.
Her husband stood by looking pale.
The midwife, by now a familiar figure, entered.
'What did you say, pains every minute?
Don't despair, we are nearly there!'
Then . . .
Cries of joy, 'It's a baby boy!'

Angela Robinson

Blind Alley

She realised, in anguish, he'd gone to 'her' . . .
Why shouldn't he? She meant nothing to him - he, too
young . . . she, too old; how can love be explained?
'What cannot be cured, must be endured', but how to live
with such pain?

In the beginning, stunned recognition.
Desolation . . . in the end.

Elizabeth Amy Johns

Firework Night At Last!

Anticipation was bubbling as she waited eagerly for the party to begin.
Smells of cooking, mixed with bonfire smoke, filled the night air. Colours vivid
brightened frosty sky, while loud bangs resounded.
Later, she found it difficult to sleep, as whirling images of colour entered her
brain.

S Mullinger

A Voice Boomed

Just before closing time two men raced
into the bank wearing comic masks. Customers
were aghast as they were commanded to lie
face-down on the floor, the robbers carelessly
gesticulating with revolvers. Loaded?
A voice boomed, 'OK everyone, cut! That's a
wrap!' And the film cameraman rolled back.

Hilary Jill Robson

The Cavemen

The men left the cave
Out they went hunting food
As they passed each other they looked
Great, in their primitive way
This was no normal day.
At last they spotted the turkeys
Each had his own pick
Food at last
It was hard in London at Christmas

Colin Allsop

From Little Acorns . . .

Autumn, early frosts and icy winds. Already the leaves on the old oak
had turned glorious shades of gold. The acorn clung firmly on; each gust
made it increasingly difficult until, finally, whoosh! it hurtled
earthwards. Rolling to a grassy hollow, safe from squirrels, hiding -
come spring, nature would intervene.

Geraldine Laker

Never To Be Forgotten?

Head first, shoulders wriggling, he inched his way out.
The passage was a tighter squeeze than he had expected.
Blinking, he emerged into the light.
Welcoming, congratulatory hands pulled him the rest of the way.
'But,' he cried, 'why did she slap my bum?'
'Ah well, forget it.'

Lee Lanciotti

Strange Catch

Fish was life, in Pintora. Daggo always dreamt of
outshining all the young men. One day he only
managed to fish out a marble-size, soft plant.
The other young men taunted him, but he was
unperturbed. The strange catch, became the
source of his good fortune; Daggo was so
famous, he won the hand of the Chief's
daughter, Nola.

Rowland Warambwa

Will The Ice Never Melt?

Hope until Millennium Eve service.
Then frozen, herded into history and present.
Old millennium's fear trembles. Foundations limiting God's
hope to the future.
Past and present's devastating seemed contradictory, false.

Yet the service was so right. God is holding us as if in ice, until we melt with a
trickling tremor of apocalyptic fear applied to the living.

R D Shooter

The Web

No trees, no green
Only a net, a web
With glued logos
Controlled minds
Brainless and greedy.
Heaps of mass produced rubbish.
A world of worthless nothing.
With heads held in the sand.
We do as they say.
Let's fight!
Let's put it right!
Let's stand proud and tall.

Joan E Blissett

Millennium, Ready Or Not!

He claimed to be the Messiah of the
final days, the ignorant crowd called
him blasphemous and bound him to a
tree, a voice in the crowd mockingly
cried 'If you're the Messiah, save
yourself!' then as if by magic his
bonds broke, then he proclaimed,
'Now has judgement come.'

Cherry

Was I The Only One

While walking past a shop, I saw a pound coin on the
pavement, so I put my foot on it then bent down to
pick it up, only to find it was made of cardboard and
stuck, can you imagine how I felt as I passed on
my way.

William Tilyard

The Final Frontier

The Journey

Early that morning we were put on the train.
When we reached our destination station we
went by road to the venue where we were
released. By tea-time we were back in our
lofts, tired but happy we had made it and
looking forward to the next pigeon race.

Diana Daley

Floor Droppings

We leave the shop, where what we have paid our money for, is swept from the
polished floor. Feeling drenched, having sat and listened to idle chatter for
what seems hours. Now lighter on the head, lighter in the pocket, this time
consuming exercise is called having a hair-do.

Leslie Holgate

The Final Frontier

Who's Chasing Who?

Apples off the back of a lorry were easy pickings, if you kept
tight to the lorry if it stopped.
I didn't, and away from the lorry, boots sounded heavy behind me.
After 15 minutes flat out, my mate called why was I running?
I then saw his new boots.

E S Segust

The Gospel

'In The Beginning'

The great train engine roared.
The machine age had begun
And wheels and engine were now one.
Designed by man. The plan,
Speed, greed and progress.
The people cheered and left the land
For something grand.
And people became slaves
To the new machines.
And progress, once a dream
Had now begun. 'Amen'.

Joan E Blissett

Our Last Meeting

She said, gulping her wine.
'Why?'
'Here's the photo taken of us last time.
Only *I* show up . . .'
Outside, I noticed -
'You have no shadow.'

Softly, he said: 'What do you see
in the wall mirror opposite?'
She saw two empty wine glasses
on a table.
'No one,' she whispered.

Chris Creedon

Hot In The Kitchen

Popping and sizzling noises were coming from the kitchen.
Speedily; on opening the door, the kitchen became a blue haze
which activated the smoke alarm.
I'd told them to 'beat it' and they had,
So I quickly poured it into the sizzling pan
and what a 'Yorkshire' that was!

Norah Page

Of Limited View

We looked to the front,
then looked to the rear, we
Looked to each side, and still
Nothing was clear. We looked
At each other - we were
Lost indeed - and though
Two heads are better than
One, or so they say, it didn't
Help a lot, until the fog
Cleared away.

Bakewell Burt

Someone Has To Get Real

The blue, flickering lights were lovely. Julie floated
And spun, helplessly. Was there anything as marvellous, as
free in her world?
A rush of air and she breathed as her brother lifted
her, then swam off.
John always seemed to be around, bringing Julie out
of fantasy and into reality.

Letty Linton

First Time

He followed the crowd. In line they neared the entrance.
It was the first time for him.
Beads of perspiration formed on his forehead.
The noise was alien to him.
Suddenly he was calm again.
The flight would not take long.
The holiday island waited four hours away.

A H Thomson

Lists

Thundering, sweating, pounding. My heart
races, body aches under the strain as I
turn to face my adversary again. Mud and
blood cake my armour and chain mail. My
horse rears under me and I set off down
the lists again, aiming my lance at my
brother knight.

John Doyle

The Final Frontier

The Mermaid

The mermaid, seated on the rock, sunlight
gleaming on her scales, singing as she
combs her long hair, sees the boat
heading towards her.
Swiftly she dives, flicking her tail,
barely a ripple as she swims into
the green depths, knowing she will be
safe from human eyes once more.

A Odger

Our Albert

That's the best I've seen you dressed our Albert. Clean shaven too.
My, you do me proud. My, you are a handsome devil.
No wonder I fell in love with you.
She kissed him on the cheek, covered his face and put the coffin lid on.

Don Goodwin

Brief Encounter

Two haddock lay side-by-side on a slab.
One said: 'We haven't met before. What's your name?'
'And we're not likely to meet again,' said the other.
'My parents must have known something when they
named me, I'm Frying Tonite.'

Kenneth Cox

Anticipation

When we get home will it be ready? All day we had waited.
If only we were closer, not long now, we must be patient, time will tell.

As we got there we knew the wait was worthwhile, for on the table
was the biggest, grandest pie you had ever seen and the smell was
magnificent, and we all tucked in with delight.

Jill K Gilbert

The Whalers

Too foreign was he in him. They knew so much about the sea,
these men of yore, husbanded in whale skin. The harbour was great
and glorious, full and fruity, as they stepped out on the stretch of
cobbles to the ship. Lord Neptune laughed to see such merriment
in youth.

Nicola Barnes

Dark

It was dark. Really, really dark. It was, in fact, the darkest dark
ever known to Man. It was so dark that only God could attempt
to comprehend it! Yes, it was that dark. Then the Lord smiled . . .
The hour had come . . . the hour when Jesus rose . . . from the dead!

Denis Martindale

Time Travel

Accomplishments by Man's endeavour,
Venturing extremities of space.
Energizing, frequency modulation.
Vastness, graces, infinity's faraway place.

A celestial vision of creation,
An illusion of planetary wealth.
Gazing upon this magnitude of knowledge,
Circling Earth's circumference, skilfully dealt.

Wondering at the complexities
Stimulating mystery.
Combining, generating courage,
Spectacle, of universal homage . . .

Lorna Tippett

None Beautiful As Janie

It was so strange, so wonderful, that feeling, falling, head over heels.
I'd hold her tightly, at night, her arm across my chest, her breath
upon my face.
Until one morning, holding her tight, pulling her to my chest, I screamed.
She'd been so beautiful.

Sandy Gunningham

The Loner

Eyes shining like beacons
Lighting his way, for he needed
No signs of arrows, blind instinct
Guided him, this lonely spirit,
Came, went, as he pleased, prowling
Watching, waiting.
Snow sent him hurrying
Towards home, hugging hedgerows,
This phantom came, squeezing
Through flap
He curled up beside his fire.

Ann Hathaway

It's A Jungle Out There

Tuning into their seductive
Screens like wolves on the
Prowl, they hunted through
The forest of digital data.
But like grazing deer they
Foraged nervously acknowledging
The wolf's territory.
Then when the wolf ventured
Too close, they leapt to the
Freedom of the off button
Ever close at hand.

Cherry

The Final Frontier

ANCHOR BOOKS SUBMISSIONS INVITED

SOMETHING FOR EVERYONE

ANCHOR BOOKS GEN - Any subject, light-hearted clean fun, nothing unprintable please.

THE OPPOSITE SEX - Have your say on the opposite gender. Do they drive you mad or can we co-exist in harmony?

THE NATURAL WORLD - Are we destroying the world around us? What should we do to preserve the beauty and the future of our planet - you decide!

All poems no longer than 30 lines.
Always welcome! No fee!
Plus cash prizes to be won!

Mark your envelope (eg *The Natural World)* And send to:
Anchor Books
Remus House, Coltsfoot Drive
Peterborough, PE2 9JX

**OVER £10,000 IN POETRY PRIZES
TO BE WON!**

Send an SAE for details on our New Year 2001 competition!

Information

We hope you have enjoyed reading this book - and that you will continue to enjoy it in the coming years.

If you like reading and writing mini sagas drop us a line, or give us a call, and we'll send you a free information pack.

Write To

Anchor Books Mini Saga Information
Remus House
Coltsfoot Drive
Woodston
Peterborough
PE2 9JX
(01733) 898102